SIX OF THE BEST
one-act plays
Nick Calderbank

Artwork by Lucy Calderbank

Special thanks to Didier Moity whose support and technical expertise has made this collection possible.

Contents

KIT KAT..6

NEXT!..18

HANKY PANKY................................31

ONLY YOU...42

TIT FOR TAT......................................66

DEJA VU...79

KIT KAT

Room. Table and chair.

RILEY *(Off)* This way, please.

JESSICA enters. Early 20's, attractive, grunge. Followed by RILEY, 40's, corporate look, suit, tie.

JESS. What's going on? What do you want? Pushing me in here like this.

RILEY. I didn't push you, madam.

JESS. I don't trust you. Who are you?

RILEY. You know who I am. Please sit down.

JESS. I don't have time for this. I've got an important appointment.

He waits. Finally, JESSICA sits.

Well ...?

RILEY. Please empty your handbag.

JESS. What! I shall do no such thing!

RILEY. We don't want to have to bring in the police, if we can possibly avoid it.

Beat. Then JESSICA opens her handbag, turns it upside down. Contents spill out onto table: purse, keys, phone, cigarettes, etc. RILEY takes bag, looks inside, opens inner pocket, removes chocolate bar, holds it up.

RILEY. What's this?

JESS. Ah, yes. My péché mignon. People are still allowed to eat chocolate, aren't they?

RILEY. Of course. But they're not allowed to steal it.

JESS. I was going to pay for it when I got to the checkout. You didn't give me a chance. You pounced on me and dragged me in here.

RILEY. In that case, why did you put it in your handbag?

JESS. I don't know. I must have spaced out. This place is so creepy. The lighting. The music. Aisle after aisle of stuff. It's like Ali Baba's cave. I'd nearly finished, just a couple more things and I was out of here. And then I saw them. My nemesis. Beckoning to me. You've heard of bulimia? It's a terrible disease. The temptation. Always gnawing away at you. I've fought against it for years. I had a moment of weakness. Of course I could have bought it. But that would have meant consciously acknowledging what I was doing. Do you see? Admitting it to myself.

RILEY considers this for a moment.

RILEY. I need to ask you a few questions.

He sits, opens his folder, takes out form.

JESS. You're new here, aren't you?

RILEY. That's right. Name?

JESS. Bennet.

RILEY. First name?

JESS. Elizabeth. My friends call me Lis. And you?

RILEY. Riley. Age?

JESS. How old do you think I am?

RILEY. Mid-twenties.

JESS. Twenty-three. I look older, don't I? How old are you?

RILEY. Please. I'll ask the questions.

JESS. You look in good shape. Do you work out?

RILEY. What's your address?

JESS. I move around a lot. "Of no fixed abode."

RILEY. Occupation?

JESS. Bit of this, bit of that. *(Winks)* Bit of the other. This is ridiculous. Don't you think? *(Indicating chocolate.)* How much do these sell for? Eighty p?

RILEY. Dickinson's operates a policy of zero tolerance.

JESS. Oh yes! Zero tolerance of a lot of things. Unions. Wage increases. Christ, this place! Someone should plant a bomb under it. Maybe *I* should ... Is she serious, you're wondering? Flaky young misfit. With moments of lucidity. So my shrink tells me. So, there's hope, she thinks. She's out of her fucking mind! Hope? Look around you. Meltdown is just around the corner. So, until then, on with the party!

She picks up the chocolate bar and removes the wrapper.

RILEY. Madam ...

JESS. "Have a break. Have a Kit Kat."

She breaks off a piece, munches it.

RILEY. You mustn't do that!

Taunting him, she holds the chocolate up before him. He tries to grab it. She twists away.

JESS. Would you care for a finger? No?

She walks about the room eating the chocolate. He stands watching her.

Yummy! Crisp. Creamy. Coated in a thick layer of smooth milk chocolate. Get one today. They're giving them away at Dickinson's. Oh, dear! All gone.

RILEY sits, takes a different form from folder, begins to fill it in.

RILEY. You shouldn't have done that.

JESS. You're right. But sometimes you have to break out. Commit some symbolic act of sabotage. Don't you feel that?

RILEY.   Now we shall have to prosecute. We have no choice.

JESS. But, Mr. Riley - where's your evidence?

RILEY points at ceiling.

JESS. Ah, yes. Video cameras. I should have known. I suppose I shall have to come clean. I'm not Elizabeth Bennet.

RILEY. You're not?

JESS. And you're not Mr. Darcy. I'm Jessica Dickinson.

RILEY. Dickinson? You mean ...?

JESS. That's right. Your boss's wayward daughter. I'm a brat. As you may have noticed. It's not uncommon, I believe. Rich man's child. I'm surprised no one warned you about me. I'm always doing things like this. Your colleagues turn a blind eye. Which is frustrating. As the whole point is to attract attention. You see, I'm a mass of contradictions. Your best bet is to forget the whole thing. Put it down to experience.

RILEY. I've filled in the forms.

JESS. Tear them up. I won't tell Daddy. Our little secret.

RILEY. I can't do that.

JESS. Why not?

RILEY. It wouldn't be right.

JESS. *Right?* Look. This is a family business. I'm an only child. One day, all this will be mine. Including the entire confectionery section.

RILEY. But it's not yours yet. The fact is you committed a crime. Willfully. It is my job to address that.

JESS. You won't have a job if you do! You don't know my father. He'd do anything to protect the family name. Dickinson's is sacred. If this comes to court, I promise you you'll be out on your ear.

RILEY. That's a risk I'll have to take. Besides, I thought you wanted to get caught.

JESS. Yes. But not to be hauled up in front of a magistrate. My face splashed all over the front pages. "Supermarket Heiress in Shoplifting Scandal." I think we got off on the wrong foot, you and I. I wonder, could you possibly...? *(She indicates video cameras)* Just for a few moments?

RILEY hesitates, then takes remote from his pocket, turns off video cameras.

Thank you. I'm sorry about all this. You're right. Time to put away childish things. *(Lowering her voice)* I have a proposal.

RILEY. Oh, yes?

JESS. Someone in my position could be very helpful to you, Mr. Riley. You'd be surprised how devoted to me my father is. In spite of my shenanigans. He's always on the lookout for good people here. I can put in a word for you. You're wasted in this kind of work. A man of your ability. You could do very well here. A management position. With corresponding salary. Company car, etc.

RILEY. You take it all for granted, don't you? People like you. There's always someone there to pick up the pieces. Sign the cheque. Have a quiet word in so-and-so's ear. You think everything's for sale, don't you? Everything and everyone.

He takes out his mobile phone. She moves close to him.

JESS. I've been a naughty girl, haven't I? Let me make it up to you. You're an attractive man. Lock the door. No one will know. I can be surprisingly discreet.

He looks at her, then moves away. He punches in number.

RILEY. Hello? Police? ... Yes, I'll hold.

JESS. Blackmail.

RILEY. I'm sorry?

JESS. Preying on young women. Planting evidence on them. Then threatening them with the police unless they agree to your terms.

RILEY. Oh, *please*!

JESS. Lunging at me.

RILEY. I was trying to stop you destroying evidence.

JESS. Groping me.

RILEY. I did not grope you! *(To telephone.)* Just a minute.

JESS. It's on the video. Your hands on me. My father has a very good lawyer. The best in the business. He runs circles round them in court. You're out on a limb. Why martyr yourself?

Beat.

RILEY *(To telephone.)* Sorry. Wrong number.

He hangs up.

JESS. Good. You did the right thing. I'll speak to my father about you. You'll do well here.

She puts her things back in her bag. Goes to leave, then stops and turns as if to speak. Thinks better of it, exits. RILEY left alone in room.

NEXT!

ALICE and MAN 1 sitting at opposite sides of small table facing each other. Both have a form in front of them. The cleaner, TONY, stands at side of stage.

MAN 1. Shall I let you into a secret? Shall I? I've chosen you. I have. Look.

He shows her his form.

See? There you are. Straight in at number one. How about that? So, all we need to know now is did you choose me? And then we're up and running. Did you? Come on, don't be coy.

MAN 1 suddenly snatches ALICE's form.

Ah-hah!

ALICE reaches for the form.

ALICE. Please ...

He withholds form.

MAN 1. What's this?

He peers at form.

"Touch him ..." Be my guest! "... large pool." The old skinny-dipping, eh? Well, all right! Let's take a closer look.

He puts on his reading glasses. ALICE again tries to snatch back her form.

MAN 1. No, you don't, young lady!

(Reads.) "I wouldn't touch him with a barge pole." Why, you little ...!

He stands threateningly. TONY takes a step forward to protect ALICE. He rings bell. MAN 1 restrains himself.

(Hisses.) Cock-teaser!

MAN 1 tears ALICE's form into tiny pieces, scatters them over her like mock confetti. Exits stage left. ALICE shaken. TONY quickly sweeps up, places a new form on the table when MAN 2 enters stage right.

MAN 2. Hello. Shall I sit here?

ALICE. Yes.

MAN 2. Lovely. Thank you very much. I popped into the supermarket on my way over here, as it happens. Two birds with one stone, as you might say. I needed to pick up a new pair of socks. This pair's on its last legs … *(laughs)* On its last legs! That's a good one! I've only had them for a couple of years. They're not made to last. That's to increase sales. I know that for a fact. Well, eventually I found the ones I wanted. But the trouble was they were in a packet of six. Six pairs. I said to the young lady there I don't want six pairs. I've only got one pair of feet.

She said, "Don't you ever change your socks?"

I said, "Of course I do. What do you take me for? I wash them overnight. That's why I buy this sort. Drip-dry."

She said, " I'm sorry we only sell them like this."

I said, "Well, I'm afraid that's not good enough." (You have to be firm with them. Stick up for your rights.) "I should like to speak to the manager," I said.

She said, "I am the manager."

Well! A young slip of a girl!

So, in the end I came away with six pairs.

TONY is getting tired of this. He yawns loudly. MAN 2 remains oblivious.

I had no choice. I can't go barefoot through the streets, can I? They've got you over a barrel.

TONY rings bell. MAN 2 stands, picks up his things.

Ooh, time's up. Come in, number two! *(laughs).* I've enjoyed our little chat. 'Bye for now.

He goes to exit, turns back.

I don't suppose I can interest you in a pair of gentleman's socks? Dark green size eleven. Brand new … Ten per cent off for quick sale? … No? Oh, well. I'll try her. *(Pointing off)*

He exits left.

(Off) Hello! Shall I sit here?

TONY sets new form for next man, stands to one side. MAN 3 enters right robotically, carrying plastic shopping bag. Sits silently slumped in chair.

ALICE. 'Evening. Nice to meet you. All right? Are you having a nice time? Good. Good. Nice place, isn't it? Yes. This is my first time here, actually. It's a good idea, isn't it? Good way of meeting people.

MAN 3 starts to remove fruit from bag, puts it on table.

You've been shopping, too, have you? You want to show me what you've bought? Bananas? Mm. Apples. Good. An apple a day. Oranges? Perfect. Get your vitamin C.

MAN 3 pulls empty bag over his head.

What are you doing? … Oh, no! Don't do that!

She grabs bag.

Oh, dear! That's for your fruit, isn't it? Let's put it back in the bag, shall we? Otherwise it'll be rolling around all over the place. Someone might slip on this *(Holding banana)*. Do themselves an injury. We'll just put it down here, shall we?

ALICE intent on replacing fruit in bag etc fails to notice MAN 3 who stands, crosses room, climbs up onto chair, peers down through open window into street below. TONY signals warning to ALICE. She looks up, sees what's happening. She rushes over, restrains MAN 3.

Careful! Careful! That's dangerous. That's quite a drop there. You could hurt yourself. Come and sit down.

She leads him back to seat. They sit.

Feeling a bit down in the dumps, are you? You've just got to hang in there. OK? Hang in there.

These words resonate with MAN 3. He looks up, tightens his tie and then, unseen by ALICE, below the level of table undoes his belt, attaches the end of his tie to the buckle, slides belt free from his trousers, and is now crouching holding end of belt looking up at ceiling for a convenient beam or hook.

Because things do get better. In time. They do. They really do. You'll see. It's like the weather. One day you'll wake up and all the clouds will have vanished. There'll be a lovely clear sky. The sun will be shining … No, no, no! Oh, God! Put your belt back on.

She jumps up, detaches belt from tie, hands belt to him.

You don't want your trousers falling down, do you? That would be really embarrassing in front of all these people.

Bell rings. MAN 3 moves away.

Wait! Look. Here's my number. Give me a call.

She scribbles telephone number on end of form, tears it off, gives it to him.

We can meet up. Have lunch or something. Go for a walk. I'd like that. All right? A friend. OK?

MAN 3 exits, TONY steering him in right direction.

See you soon!

ALICE is left emotionally exhausted. TONY sets new forms, etc. MAN 4 bounds on stage right.

MAN 4. Hello, hello, hello!

He does a little jig. Interrupted by MAN 1 re-entering stage left.

MAN 1. Hang about, sunshine!

ALICE wheels round.

(To ALICE.) A word in your ear, darlin'. Her over there. Number six. She is to die for. Tits out to here. Makes you look like the dog's dinner. And she is all over me. Gimme her phone number just like that. Thought you'd like to know. *(To MAN 4.)* She's all yours, mate.

MAN 1 goes to exit. TONY "accidentally" trips him up. He falls, gets up glowering. TONY feigns apology. MAN 1 exits.

MAN 4 tries to recover his momentum. He completes his jig.

MAN 4. ... Olé! Six brothers and sisters I had. Six of them. That's how I learned to dance. Waiting for the bathroom! I've got a confession to make. When I was young, I felt like a man trapped in a woman's body. Then I was born! No, but to be frank I'm not the world's greatest lover. I'm not ...

ALICE leaps up.

ALICE. Oi! Stop it!

MAN 4. *Eh?*

ALICE. I didn't come here tonight to listen to this.

MAN 4. No, but listen. I once caught a Peeping Tom …

ALICE. I don't care.

MAN 4. And he was booing me!

ALICE. I don't care, I tell you ! I don't care about Peeping Toms. Or any other of the figments of your smutty imagination. It bores me to tears!

MAN 4 gives her a hurt look, slinks off stage. ALICE sits, does deep-breathing exercises in effort to calm herself. TONY approaches.

TONY. You all right?

ALICE looks up. She nods.

You haven't found him yet?

ALICE. Who?

TONY. Mr. Right.

ALICE. I'm beginning to think he doesn't exist.

ALICE turns away despondently. TONY whips off his cleaner's coat and cap to reveal smart DJ underneath. We now see he is a strikingly handsome young man.

He hands her his card with a flourish.

ALICE looks up, startled by the unexpected transformation.

TONY. Tony Wright at your service.

ALICE. No!

TONY. I know, what are the chances?

ALICE. *(Laughing)* Alice Mackenzie.

TONY. Enchanté.

They shake hands. A powerful current passes between them. They begin to dance, singing opening lines of "Cheek to Cheek":

"Heaven, I'm in heaven. And my heart beats so that I can hardly speak ... etc."

The dance ends. TONY whispers in ALICE's ear. She nods giggling. They begin to tiptoe away. As they leave ALICE calls out to MAN 3 off.

ALICE. Call me! Don't forget.

The stage is empty. Beat. TONY returns, rings bell, runs off. Enter MAN 5. He sits, looks around for ALICE. Notices a captive audience watching. His eyes light up. He jumps up, crosses downstage. Goes into his spiel.

MAN 5. What is Bimbo? ... I mean, Kimbo. *(s.v.)* Damn, gotta get that right!

Points to his Kimbo badge ("What is KIMBO?")

I'm glad you asked me that. Two years ago, like a lot of people - maybe some of you here tonight - I was stuck in a rut. And then one day-

Off Loud hooter sounds followed by voice "Next!"

Deflated, MAN 5 exits.

HANKY PANKY

Party: guests chatting, drinking, flirting, etc.

ROBBIE wearing kilt dances Scottish jig. Applause.

MARGARET, hostess, circulates amongst guests with nibbles. ROBBIE exchanges a few words with her as she passes. MARGARET blushes.

RICHARD eyes JACK and SUZY dancing a slow smoochy dance.

SUZY *(S. voce.)* I want you.

JACK *(Ibid.)* I want you.

SUZY. I mean, now.

JACK. Now? But, how ...?

SUZY. The bedroom.

JACK. What if someone comes in?

SUZY. They can join in.

JACK. All right.

SUZY. I'll go first. You count to 30. Then follow me.

SUZY exits. JACK starts mentally counting.

      *   *   *

JENNY and MERVIN dancing together .

JENNY. I like older men.

MERV. Do you?

JENNY. Not old men. They're creepy! Drooling all over you. But older men. I like them. They know what a woman likes.

MERV. And they've got the money to give it to her.

      *   *   *

MARGARET. I can't think where Ronald's got to. He said he'd be back ages ago.

ROBBIE. He'll be all right. Probably detained at the nineteenth hole.

MARGARET. You see, I can't really serve the food until he gets here. People must be starving.

ROBBIE. Dinnae fash yersel', Margaret. They're havin' a great time. Gettin' fou and unco' happy!

* * *

JACK goes to leave. RICHARD arrives.

RICHARD. Ah, Jack ...

JACK. Hello, Richard.

RICHARD. Having fun?

JACK. Yes, thanks.

RICHARD. Good, good. Just a quick word about the Renault contract, if I may.

JACK. The thing is, Richard ...

RICHARD. Won't take a sec'. Now, our best bet, as I see it ...

* * *

JENNY. Have you ...?

MERV. Have I what?

JENNY. Got a lot of money?

MERV. Oodles of it. And I like to spend it.

JENNY. Can't take it with you, can you?

They dance.

* * *

ROBBIE. Golf? *(Dismissive gesture)* Now, tossing the caber ... That's a real test of a man's mettle. We're a hardy race, Margaret. Virile. And that creates jealousy. When I'm walkin' down the street here in London, in the kilt, I know what everyone's thinkin'!

* * *

SUZY returns, pissed off. RICHARD completes his briefing, smiles at SUZY, leaves.

SUZY. Where were you?

JACK. Richard captured me.

SUZY. Richard?

JACK. He's my boss. I couldn't afford to offend him.

SUZY. It's OK to offend me?

JACK. That's not fair!

SUZY. It's not about fairness, Jack. It's about getting what you want. The garden shed. We'll do it there.

JACK. Outside?

SUZY. Yes, outside.

JACK. I'll check it out.

Exit JACK.

*   *   *

ROBBIE hands MARGARET folded sheet of paper.

MARGARET. Thank, you, Robbie. What is it?

ROBBIE. It's a wee poem I wrote.

MARGARET. Ah. Lovely.

ROBBIE. It's for you, Margaret. Read it.

MARGARET. Right.

MARGARET reads.

(Shocked.) Oh, Robbie!

ROBBIE. I mean it. Every word.

MARGARET. Oh, dear.

* * *

MERV. Do you like to travel, Jennifer?

JENNY. I love it! You know where I've always dreamed of going? Barbados.

MERV. Ah, yes!

JENNY. Elton John's got a villa out there. And so has Cliff Richard.

* * *

JACK returns.

JACK. It's full of stuff. Up to the ceiling.

SUZY. We'll do it standing up. Like Marlon Brando and wossername in Last Tango in Paris.

JACK. I missed that one. Anyway, it's started to rain.

SUZY. Look, are you sure you're up for this?

JACK. Of course I am. What about the bathroom?

SUZY. OK. I'll see you there in 2 minutes.

JACK. Right.

SUZY. And don't be late!

Exit SUZY.

                *   *   *

MERV. It's funny you should say that. I happen to be planning a trip to the Caribbean myself. Taking in all the islands. Including Barbados.

JENNY. You're so lucky!

MERV. Perhaps you'd like to come with me?

JENNY. *Me?*

MERV. I'm very intuitive. About people. I'm sure you'd make the perfect travelling companion. First-class all the way. The best hotels. Private beaches. Rum and Coke on tap. We could drop in on Elton if he's in residence.

JENNY. Do you know him?

MERV. We go back a long way. Lovely man. Get him to sing something for you. *(Sings softly.)* "It seems to me that you live your life like a candle in the wind!"

MERV and JENNY dance. JACK exits.

MERV. Think about it. There are two types of people in this world. Right? Number one: Those who stay at home dreaming. And number two: Those who go out there and make their dreams come true! I think I know which type you are, Jennifer.

Loud thump and cry off.

MARGARET. Goodness gracious!

GUEST. What was that?

Dancers stop dancing, etc. JACK enters clutching his eye, followed by RICHARD.

RICHARD. Are you all right, old boy?

JACK. No problem.

MARGARET. Are you sure?

JACK. Yes, I'm fine, thanks. Really.

RICHARD and MARGARET leave, party resumes. SUZY enters.

SUZY. What happened to you?

JACK. I was there. I was just checking to make sure you were inside. And Richard came bursting out. Sent me flying!

SUZY. You idiot!

JACK. What?

SUZY. I meant the bathroom upstairs.

JACK. They've got two? How was I supposed to know?

SUZY. I indicated to you with a little jerk of my head.

JACK. I thought that was just a nervous tic.

SUZY stares at him. Turns, stalks away. RICHARD starts to chat her up. JACK starts drinking.

JACK. Same old Merv! Up to your old tricks again, are you?

MERV. Shut up, Wilson!

JACK. "First-class all the way"? That's a joke!

MERV. Don't listen to him. He's drunk.

JACK. Gonna introduce you to his famous pals? Where's he gonna take you? Bangkok?

MERV. I'm warning you!

JACK. You know what they call him?

MERV. Shut your filthy mouth!

JACK. "Merv the Perv"!

MERVIN throws himself at JACK. MARGARET tries to intervene. Other guests react. At this moment the door opens: Ronnie, returning from his game of golf, stands in the doorway observing the pandemonium before him.

ONLY YOU

SCENE ONE

Living room. Framed reproduction of Picasso's "The Dove" on wall. STEVE and LIS. She is standing wearing overcoat with suitcase.

STEVE. I can do better. I can. Listen to you. I mean, really listen. With ... what's it called? Empathy. I can learn to do that. And share things with you. My insecurities. My fears and so on. Of course, this is my worst fear. This is a nightmare! Why are you doing this? We've had a good marriage, haven't we? We've had our ups and downs. But we've come through. We respect and we care for each other. Isn't that true?

LIS. Yes.

STEVE. So could you please explain why in heaven's name you are doing this!

LIS. I need something else.

STEVE. What?

LIS. I don't know. I have to find out.

STEVE. You don't know? You mean, you're ready to turn your back on a perfectly good marriage and take a leap in the dark? But that's madness!

LIS. No, it's not. There's a whole world out there.

STEVE. There's a whole world in here. Is there someone else?

LIS. No.

STEVE. That chap you got in to fix the loo because I couldn't do it?

LIS. There's no one else.

STEVE. What'll I do here on my own?

LIS. The same kind of thing you do now, I expect. Read. Watch television. Potter around, making cups of tea.

STEVE. But you won't be there.

LIS. No. You can get out more.

STEVE. Where? Go to the pub and drown my sorrows? Or just drown myself? Get it over with.

LIS. Steve! You'll be able to do all sorts of things. Without having to worry about me all the time.

STEVE. What things?

LIS. All those things you used to do. Play cricket.

STEVE. At my age?

LIS. Well, tennis then. People play tennis till they drop. Keep up with people.

STEVE. What people?

LIS. Your friends. Your old friends. You have to get out there. Or life will pass you by. You can try online dating.

STEVE. I'm not interested in finding someone else. It's you I want. Is that what you do? Online dating?

LIS. No.

STEVE. What about the kids? Have you discussed this with them?

LIS. I mentioned it to Matt.

STEVE. "Mentioned it"? Did he give you the thumbs-up?

LIS. He didn't take sides.

STEVE. What about Rachel?

LIS. You should speak to them yourself.

STEVE. How long have you been feeling like this?

LIS. Some time now.

STEVE. Why didn't you talk to me about it?

LIS. I have.

STEVE. Yes, but this is different. This is you standing there with a suitcase. About to walk out of my life. So, please. Bear with me. Talk to me now.

LIS. It's too late.

STEVE. No, it's not. We can fix this.

LIS. It's not something that can be fixed.

STEVE. Anything can be fixed. We'll talk this thing out. Really get to the bottom of it.

LIS. I'm going.

She stands.

STEVE. Don't! Not yet.

LIS. My cab will be here any minute.

STEVE. He'll ring the bell. Please.

Reluctantly, she sits.

Is this about sex?

LIS. It's not about any one thing.

STEVE. I try to give you pleasure.

LIS. And you do. It's just that it's the same pleasure over and over. Like eating the same meal every day.

STEVE. I'd be happy to do that.

LIS. Really?

STEVE. If I like something, it's for life.

LIS. We're so different.

STEVE. That's the secret of our success. I've always been faithful, you know. Sounds so old-fashioned, doesn't it? All this time. Only you. And it's not as if I haven't had opportunities.

LIS. I don't doubt it. You're an attractive man.

STEVE. But not to you. You're the only woman I've ever wanted. It's true. And now you want to leave me.

LIS. I have to.

STEVE. I was smitten. You have no idea. It seemed hopeless. You were out of my league. I told Jerry how I felt about you. He said, "Ask her out. She can only say no." The following morning at school during break I saw you go into the photocopying room. So I took a deep breath and followed you in. We were alone in there.

"Look here," I said.

You looked up as if trying to place me.

"Perhaps we might have a drink together? You and me. Sometime. When you're free. If you'd like to do that."

Somehow I managed to stop babbling.

You blinked. And then you smiled.

"Why not?" you said. Bless you!

Do you remember?

LIS. Yes.

STEVE. So we had our drink. And we found we liked each other. We clicked. We discovered we're both film buffs. We had a similar sense of humour. I made you laugh with my imitation of the head. The following week we had dinner. And then sometime later, on a wet Sunday afternoon, we returned bedraggled from our walk to my tiny bedsit. And to my joy quite openly you began to peel off your wet things. And so I did the same. And with the rain lashing down on the roof above our heads we made love. And I can honestly say it was the most transcendental experience of my life.

Of course I was convinced it couldn't last. How could it? And yet it did. It was obvious what I saw in you. What you saw in me, that was the mystery.

LIS. You touched me.

STEVE. Did I? Perhaps you don't like me any more?

LIS. That's not true.

STEVE. The same old routines. Day in, day out. My jokes. My rants. You've heard them all a thousand times.

LIS. You talk as if you had one foot in the grave.

STEVE. I'm not young, am I?

LIS. You're somewhere in between.

STEVE. No man's land.

LIS. I can't be your crutch. It's not fair to expect that. What about my life?

STEVE. It's our life.

LIS. No, it's not! We're two different people.

STEVE. What about the house?

LIS. We can sell it.

STEVE. I'm not selling it. You might change your mind.

She shakes her head.

How do you know? You might miss me.

LIS. Of course I'll miss you. But I won't be coming back.

STEVE. You sound very sure of yourself.

LIS. I am.

STEVE. You never know. I never thought you'd agree to go out with me. But you did. And we married and we had two wonderful children and a home and a whole life together.

LIS. *Don't.*

STEVE. Where will you go?

LIS. I'll stay with Maggie till I find somewhere.

STEVE. Ah, yes, Maggie. I should have known. This is her idea, isn't it?

LIS. We talked about the situation.

STEVE. Of course. She's always been jealous. Poisoning you against me. With her snide little remarks. And you let her. How could you do that?

LIS. It's my decision.

STEVE *(Indicating their home.)* Does all this mean nothing to you?

LIS. Please. Do you think this is easy for me?

STEVE. Then stay! Stay with me. You're the love of my life. Without you I'm nothing. With you I can do anything. Anything!

LIS. But you don't! That's the reality. You stopped doing things years ago.

STEVE. A fresh start. That's what we need. We'll relocate. Somewhere in the south. Spain. Why not? You love Spain. We'll sell up here and buy a villa on the coast. Down in Andalusia. It's beautiful down there. We'll go to the beach every day. We'll swim, and lie in the sun. And read novels. And drink wine. And make love. The way we used to. Do you remember? We couldn't keep our hands off each other. It was incredible! And I'll start writing again. I'll dig out that book I was working on. I'll finish it. You can help me. Give me invaluable editorial advice.

She stands.

Stay.

LIS. I can't. I'm suffocating here. I've got to get out. Where's that cab? He should have been here ages ago. You didn't ...? You cancelled it, didn't you?

STEVE. I had to.

LIS. You bastard!

STEVE. I couldn't let you go.

LIS. I'll call Matt. He'll come and fetch me. Or Maggie.

She rummages in her bag.

Where's my phone? Did you take my phone? You-give me that back! How dare you! You thief! Stealing my things!

She starts to hit him. He takes the blows. Finally, exhausted, she stops.

I'll bloody well walk to the station!

She goes to the door. Finds it's locked.

STEVE. I have to do this. Because if you go, you may never come back. And I know you'd live to regret that as much as I would. This is where you belong. Here. With me.

SCENE TWO

The same. Minutes later. LIS seated arms folded.

STEVE. Do you remember the time we went to Paris? Our second honeymoon. We left the kids with my mum and dad. On our own again at last. We stayed in that little hotel in the Latin Quarter. And we saw that wonderful exhibition. Monet, wasn't it?

LIS. Manet.

STEVE. Manet, of course. And that amazing place we went to for dinner on the second night. "Chez Flo"! That was it. And when the waiter came I ordered for us in my best French. He listened to me patiently. And then replied in impeccable English! And you had snails, didn't you? And you insisted I try one. And it was so good I ended up scoffing the lot! And later walking hand in hand along the banks of the Seine. Wasn't it magical? Paris! What a city. So many beautiful women! But the most beautiful woman of all was the one who was with me.

LIS. That was thirty years ago.

STEVE. You're still a knockout. Even today I can't take my eyes off you. Why don't we do it again? Go back there. A third honeymoon. Why not? What's stopping us? Jump on the next Eurostar?

LIS. You seem to have forgotten: I'm leaving you.
STEVE. A final fling. Eh? What about it? Then, when we get back, we can re-assess the situation.

LIS. I told you. I've made up my mind.

STEVE. Now you listen to me. OK? You have something that your pal Maggie could never have. A marriage that has stood the test of time. That's rare these days. It's precious. You don't just toss it away on a whim. And when things start to get a bit rough, you don't abandon ship. You get your head down, and you weather the storm. You come through.

Pause.

There is someone else, isn't there?

LIS. No!

STEVE. It is that handyman guy. I'm sure of it.

LIS. Don't be ridiculous.

STEVE. The snake!

LIS. He's actually very nice. You'd like him.

STEVE. Really? Got a lot in common, have we? We're both fucking my wife?

LIS grabs door key and runs towards door. STEVE stops her. They struggle.

Give me that!

LIS. Get your hands off me!

He recovers key.

STEVE. You're not going anywhere! Now, sit down there!

He pushes her onto seat.

LIS. This is so not you.

STEVE. Isn't it?

LIS. It's over, Steve. Don't you see? I don't love you any more.

Beat. Doorbell rings. LIS jumps up.

LIS. That must be the cab.

She crosses to window.

STEVE. No. It's that chap who does the garden.

STEVE unlocks door. Steps out into hall.

JACK *(Off)* Sorry to bother you, sir. I mowed the lawn. And I finished the weedin'. Before I go, I wonder if I could trouble you for a glass of water?

STEVE *(Ibid)* Of course.

STEVE re-enters followed by JACK.

STEVE. I'm just going to get a glass of water for ...

JACK. Jacko, sir. That's what people calls me.

STEVE. Right. I won't be a moment.

STEVE exits. JACK hovers in entrance to living room. Removes his hat.

JACK. I'm sorry to intrude upon you like this, madam.

LIS. Not at all. Come in.

JACK. I wouldn't want to get mud on your carpet.

LIS. Don't worry about that.

JACK enters room.

LIS. Please. Sit down.

JACK. If I may just for a moment.

JACK sits.

I gets these little spells. If I'd known I was goin' to last this long, I'd have taken better care of meself! *(Laughs)* I'm on me own now, you see. I had the misfortune to lose my lady wife durin' the lockdown.

LIS. It must have been hard for you.

JACK. It was, madam. We'd just celebrated our golden weddin' anniversary when she was taken poorly. A week later she was gone.

LIS. I'm so sorry.

JACK. The good Lord giveth and He taketh away. She's in my thoughts all the time, my Bess. I still talk to her, you know. You probably think I'm mad.

LIS. Not at all.

JACK. It's like she's still there. I ask her advice. Like "How long should I boil the sprouts for?" You know, silly little things like that. Or "What time does the bus go to Swaffam ?" And she'll tell me. In my 'ead, like. Oh, yes. I could never let 'er go.

STEVE returns with tea, etc.

STEVE. I thought you might like a cup of tea?

JACK. You shouldn't have gone to all that trouble on my account.

STEVE. We were ready for one ourselves, weren't we, darling?

Business serving tea. Jack drinks.

JACK. Nice cup o' tea, that, sir!

LIS. Do have a piece of cake.

JACK. Don't mind if I do.

He takes a bite.

Did you make this cake yourself, by any chance, madam?

LIS. I did.

JACK. Well, allow me to congratulate you. It's scrumptious! There's no other word for it.

LIS. Thank you.

JACK. My Bess made a lovely carrot cake. I hope you don't mind me goin' on about her?

LIS. Not at all.

JACK. I won't pretend we never had a cross word. We'd have "an exchange of views," as they say. And then we'd look at each other and we'd both burst out laughin'. We'd have a little cuddle and a cup o' tea - as we are now - and we'd be right as rain again! We both said our piece - and then we made our peace. That's how I like to put it. We'd 'ave a good laugh, too. What's the difference between England's football team and a teabag?

STEVE. I don't know.

JACK. The teabag stays in the cup longer!

STEVE and LIS laugh.

JACK. That was one of her favourites. (S*ings.*) "When you're smiling ... etc."

STEVE and LIS join in at first self-consciously then with enthusiasm.

STEVE. I must say, you're a real tonic, Jacko! I'm Steve, by the way.

LIS. And I'm Lis.

STEVE. Would you care to stay for lunch?

JACK. Oh, now I wouldn't want to put you out, Steve.

STEVE. We were going to have a bite anyway, weren't we, darling? It'll just be some cold meat and salad.

JACK. I wouldn't say no. Thank you kindly.

LIS. Right, then. Won't be long.

STEVE. I'll give you a hand.

JACK. I'll just sit here and have 40 winks, if I may?

STEVE. Of course. Make yourself at home. See you in a bit.

LIS and STEVE exit. As soon as the coast is clear, JACK leaps into action. Examines picture hanging on wall.

JACK *(Dropping his countryman accent)* A Picasso! And they ain't even fitted an alarm system! Some people!

He takes down picture, turns it over, removes "original" from frame. Replaces it with another reproduction he takes out of his duffel bag.

JACK. Amazon. Seven pound ninety-nine!

He then rolls up "original", puts it in his bag and re-hangs picture.

They'll never know the difference!

He looks round for an exit. Sees window. Turns to leave. Stops, grabs another slice of cake, crams it into his mouth.

Tally-ho!

He exits through window.

Beat.

STEVE *(Off, whistling)* "When you're smiling ..."

He and LIS enter with tray with food, wine, etc.

STEVE. Where is he? *(Calls.)* Jacko!

LIS. His bag and hat are gone.

STEVE. That's funny.

LIS. Perhaps he had to go. Preferred to slip away- quietly.

STEVE. Wonderful old character!

LIS. We shall have to look him up.

STEVE. We shall. You and me, then?

LIS. Yes. I just said that about not loving you any more to make you let me go. You know that, don't you? Now I find I don't want to go after all.

STEVE reaches out and squeezes LIS's hand.

STEVE. Your were right. I'm too stuck in my ways. I should get out more. I'll fish out my tennis raquet. Start playing again. You should unpack.

LIS. Unless ...

STEVE *(Alarmed)* Yes?

LIS.   You still fancy that weekend in Paris?

STEVE smiles. He checks train times etc on his mobile.

STEVE. Can we make the four-thirty Eurostar?

LIS. If we hurry.

STEVE. All right, then!

He makes booking.

Voilà!

LIS. I'll wrap this *(ie, lunch)*. We can have it on the way.

STEVE. And I'll go and pack a few things.

LIS. Et on y va.

STEVE. Dinner Chez Flo!

He kisses her.

Oh, yes ...

He hands her her mobile phone.

LIS. Thanks.

STEVE exits. LIS notices the picture on the wall is squint. She straightens it and begins to wrap food.

TIT FOR TAT

Male actor plays the male roles, female actor both female roles.

Table for two in restaurant.
Enter HENRY and MIA.

HENRY *(To WAITRESS off.)* This table here? Right.

They sit face to face.

So ... this is very pleasant.

MIA. Yes.

HENRY. It's good to unwind after a hard day ... Do you know "Bentley's"?

MIA. No, this is the first time I've been here, actually.

HENRY. I think you'll like it. I can recommend the lamb. It's generally quite good.

MIA. I'm a vegetarian.

HENRY. Ah. I see. Well, I expect they can fix you some sort of salad ... Excuse me, I must just ...

He gets out his mobile phone, begins to write email. She pours glasses of water. Waits. Eventually she gets out her mobile. He sends his email, puts his mobile on table beside him. Waits. She finally puts her mobile on table. He reaches over, takes her mobile, places it on his side of table.

Let's put this here, shall we? Out of temptation's way.

MIA. *What?!*

HENRY. When someone takes you out to dinner, it's polite to give him a modicum of your attention.

MIA. What about you? You started it. Sitting there texting away!

HENRY. For your information, I was not "texting". I had to send a very important email. To Hollywood ...

She reaches over, takes his mobile and places it on table beside her.

HENRY. *Hey!*

MIA. All right, then. Let's put *this* here.

HENRY. You give that back!

MIA. Sorry.

HENRY. I happen to be expecting a very important call later this evening.

MIA shrugs. HENRY leans over and seizes her scarf.

MIA. Hoi! That's Gucci!

He holds it out of arm's reach.

HENRY. Gucci, Gucci, goo!

She sneezes into her napkin, then hurls it at him.

Ugh!

He picks up his glass and pours water over her head. She kicks him under table.

Ah! Look! Blood!

MIA. A tiny scratch. You can hardly see it.

HENRY. You should be locked up. You ... barbarian!

He gets up, limps out of the room. She retrieves her scarf and mobile, dries her face with HENRY's napkin, relaxes. Looks about her. His mobile phone, still on the table beside her, rings. She picks it up.

MIA. Hello? ... No, I'm afraid he's been called away ... Thank you ... I'm here all on my own ... I know. Sad, isn't it? ... "Bentley's"... That would be nice. See you in a bit.

She hangs up. Smiles to herself. Takes pocket mirror from her bag, checks her makeup, etc. Puts it back.

(To WAITRESS off) Waitress! A Kir, please. Thank you.

After a short while, BUD, a tipsy American, enters.

BUD. Howdy!

MIA *(Aside to audience.)* Hollywood? ... Oh, my God! It's Clint! Clint Eastwood! *(All a-flutter, half rising)* Hello.

BUD. OK if I ...?

MIA. Of course.

BUD. Great!

He sits opposite her.

MIA. You were quick!

BUD. Quick on the draw, that's me. "Bang! Bang!" How ya doin'?

MIA. Fine, thank you.

BUD. Ain't I seen you somewhere before?

MIA. I don't think so.

BUD. Weren't you in that movie? "8 Heads in a Duffel Bag"?

MIA. I'm not an actor.

BUD. Well, if you ain't, ya should be!

MIA. Thank you.

BUD. 'Cos you got it, baby. I'm tellin' ya. Chick like you? Big time! ... Nice place.

MIA. Yes, it is. The lamb is good here. Generally.

BUD. You look good enough to eat yourself, young lady! I mean, look at ya! Jeez Louise!

His mobile rings. BUD picks up, turns away, speaking quietly.

BUD. Hi, honey ... Yeah, yeah. I'm sorry. I didn't have time to call ya.

MIA. Excuse me.

MIA gets up, goes to exit to 'loo. Then stops, eavesdropping.

BUD *(Still on mobile)* I'm still stuck here at the office ... I know, I know.

MIA. *(To audience.)* Oh, the little liar! It can't be Clint. He's too much of a gentleman.

She exits.

BUD. This big contract came in late this afternoon ... Yeah. Look, don't wait up for me, OK? ... I love you, honey.

WAITRESS enters. Serves MIA'S Kir. Places menus on her side of table.

WAIT. Excuse me, sir.

BUD. Yeah?

WAIT. You are ...?

BUD. What?

WAIT. I mean, what is your name, sir?

BUD. Mister Man.

WAIT I'm sorry, we have no reservation tonight for a Mr Mann.

BUD. Don't tell me ya gotta make a reservation to eat in this crummy joint!

WAIT. I'm afraid I shall have to ask you to leave, sir.

BUD *(Mincing voice.)* "I'm afraid I shall have to ask you to leave, sir!"

WAITRESS Signals to bouncer.

Don't get your knickers in a twist, lady! I'm outa here. Uptight little dyke! (*Blows raspberry*)

WAITRESS watches him leave. She shakes her head. Business straightening chair, etc.

(To audience.) You get all sorts round here. Saturday night. They've had a drink. Some of them can get a bit stroppy. Ejecting undesirables. It's all part of the job.

She exits. HENRY re-enters. He looks about. MIA returns.

MIA. Oh, hello.

HENRY *(Sheepishly.)* Hello.

MIA. You forgot your phone.

HENRY. Yes.

She hands him phone.

Thank you.

MIA. How's your leg?

HENRY. Not too bad. I hope you managed to dry off?

She nods.

Good. Look, I'm sorry about ...

MIA. That's OK.

HENRY. No, I behaved very badly. I flew off the handle.

MIA. Me, too.

HENRY Yes, exactly! "Me Too." We've got to pull our socks up, haven't we? Perhaps we could start over again?

MIA. All right.

He pulls back her chair for her.

MIA. Thank you.

She sits. He sits.

HENRY. If I may say so, you're looking particularly attractive this evening, Miss Robinson.

MIA. Please. Call me Mia.

HENRY. Henry.

They beam at each other.

MIA *(Aside to audience.)* He's not such a bad bloke after all!

HENRY. Waitress! A bottle of champagne, please!

They chuckle about their recent squabble. At which point Henry's business associate whom Mia spoke to earlier on HENRY'S mobile enters. He sees the couple in tête à tête, turns and quietly leaves as HENRY and MIA lean in closely towards each other, speaking softly now.

DEJA VU

SCENE 1

Paris street.
MAY wearing shades sitting at table outside on pavement writing postcards. JACK enters. Passing he sees MAY, does double take. His face lights up. He stops, approaches her.

JACK. C'est pas vrai! *May!*

MAY turns.

It is! It is you. Oh, my God! I thought I'd never see you again.

MAY. I'm sorry. I think you must be confusing me with someone else.

JACK. I'd know you anywhere. It's me: Jack. It's so wonderful to see you. You look great. You haven't changed. If anything, you're even more beautiful now than you were then!

MAY. Jack?

JACK. You don't recognise me? I've put on weight, I know. And of course I'm older. Here. I've got a photo. Of us. Together.

JACK fumbles for his wallet. Takes out passport photo, shows it to May.

It's a bit tatty now. I've been carrying it around ever since. Look.

MAY peers at it sceptically.

MAY. That's us?

JACK. Yes!

MAY. Are you sure?

JACK. Can't you see? I had a beard then. But you can still see it's me. I mean, look at that nose!

MAY. I'd never wear that colour.

JACK. It's you, May. You and me. And look how happy we are together!

MAY. When did you say this was?

JACK. A long time ago now. It seemed as if everything was possible. Everything and anything. The tango. The "figures" we invented. We made tango "cool". That's what people said. You were a natural. Did you keep it up?

MAY. No. No, I didn't.

JACK. That's a shame. You were so good.

MAY. Were we ...?

JACK. Oh, yes! It was incredible! It was as if there was some force pulling us together. And then suddenly you left. You had to return to London. Some kind of family crisis. I went with you to the airport. You told me you'd be back as soon as you could. At the check-in we embraced. It was only then as you were about to go through customs that I realised we hadn't exchanged phone numbers! I called out. "Wait!" I scribbled my number on a scrap of paper and held it out to you. "Call me when you get to London," I said. You nodded. You blew me a kiss. Then you disappeared. And that was the last I saw of you until today. I waited. And I waited. But I never received that phone call. You have no recollection of this?

MAY. I've had some health problems in the last few years.

JACK. Oh, I'm sorry to hear that. Yes, well, as time passed I began to give up hope. Our love affair took on the quality of a dream. But here you are again! You're not a dream. You're real. You've come back.

He reaches out, grasps her hand.

SCENE 2

Inside JACK'S flat. Sound off of JACK and MAY climbing stairs.

JACK *(off)* Nearly there! Sixième étage sans acenseur. Keeps you fit. Either that or it finishes you off!

Sound off of JACK unlocking door to flat. JACK and MAY enter.

Voilà! Chez moi.

MAY looks around.

Do you remember it?

MAY. I don't know. It's charming.

MAY walks around room. She crosses to window. looks out.

And what a wonderful view! The Eiffel Tower. You're so lucky! Living here in the heart of Paris.

She looks at paintings on wall.

Did you do these? They're very good, Jack.

JACK. It's my métier. That's how we met. Up in Montmartre. Where all the portrait painters work. And you chose me. And you sat there while I painted your portrait.

MAY. How romantic!

JACK. It was. Please. Make yourself at home.

MAY sits on sofa. JACK goes into his send-up of French waiter.

Un petit apéritif, Madame?

MAY. Oui. S'il vous plait.

JACK. Un petit Kir? Allez.

JACK serves MAY with a flourish. They chink glasses.

MAY. Les yeux dans les yeux.

JACK. You remember that?

MAY. It's something people say, isn't it? Where's the cat?

JACK. Pablo? He died. He was getting on. So you remember him?

MAY All artists have cats, don't they?

JACK. And the Mont St. Michel? And St. Malo?

MAY. St. Malo? Yes. Mussels. Huge bowls of steaming mussels. They were so good!

JACK. You see? It's coming back to you.

JACK joins MAY on sofa.

How wonderful bumping into each other again like this! Of course, I know nothing of your life since then. For all I know you may be happily married.

MAY shakes her head.

Forgive me. I had to ask. I've missed you. So much. You know, sometimes - if you're incredibly lucky - you get a second chance. We could be so happy. Here. Together.

MAY. I'm fifty-five, Jack.

JACK. The perfect age. That's when life begins.

May laughs.

MAY. My French is terrible.

JACK. You'd pick it up. It's easy. Just keep on saying "Oh, là, là! J'en ai marre!" You could give it a try. If it doesn't work out, then no hard feelings.

MAY. You know, I'm almost tempted.

JACK. What did Oscar Wilde say? "I can resist anything except temptation."

SCENE 3

JACK and MAY strolling in public park.

MAY. I think that was probably the best meal I've ever eaten! Thank you, Jack.

HE kisses her lightly on the cheek, takes her hand. They walk hand in hand.

JACK. My pleasure. "Chez Flo". It hasn't changed. Nor have the waiters. Did you hear what Marcel said when he saw us? "Ah, bonjour, les amants! Comment ca va?"

MAY. Did he?

JACK. You remember the last time we went there? I ordered snails. And you pulled a face. And when they arrived I made you try one. And you loved it! In the end you had my snails and I had your egg mayonnaise.

MAY laughs.

MAY. I've always been greedy.

JACK. That's not greed. It's enjoying the good things in life.

They walk.

MAY. I don't know, Jack. This plan of yours, it's such a leap in the dark!

JACK. That's what makes it so exciting!

MAY. Would we get on together?

JACK. I'm pretty easy-going.

MAY. I'm not! I've got all sorts of hang-ups. I'm what's it called? OCD. Everything at home has to be neat and tidy.

JACK. Very sensible.

MAY. I can't be expected to stay out till all hours. I must get my sleep.

JACK. "Chief nourisher in life's feast."

MAY. You see how boring I am?

JACK. Endlessly fascinating!

MAY. And I'm a terrible cook.

JACK. No worries. I love to cook!

MAY. What about my things? I can't live without them.

JACK. We'll hire a van and bring them over.

MAY. Will there be room for them? I mean, my clothes alone ...

JACK. There's bags of room. I'm looking forward to this!

They sit on bench.

MAY. It would be a real test. I'm panicking already! I failed my driving test three times.

JACK. Still, you got there in the end.

MAY. I didn't. I gave up.

JACK. Ah, well. You can't win 'em all.

MAY. I mean, honestly, Jack. I hardly know anything about you. Are you English or are you French? Are you Jack or are you Jacques?

JACK. I'm a mongrel. "Lady and the Tramp."

MAY. Seriously. You say we met before but I have no clear memory of that.

JACK. May. The past is past. It's over. Gone. What matters is the present and the future. The important thing is that we're here now. You and me. Together. There's no doubt about that, is there?

HE kisses her. She responds.

MAY. Oh, Jack!

JACK. If you really want something badly enough, then you can make it happen. I honestly believe that.

MAY stands.

MAY. I'm sorry. I'm exhausted. All that wine. I'm not used to it. I need an early night.

JACK. Yes. Get a good night's sleep. You'll feel better in the morning. Come over tomorrow. We'll have breakfast together. I'll walk you to your hotel.

MAY. Don't bother. It's just round the corner.

He embraces her.

JACK. Goodnight, my darling. I love you.

He kisses her. She murmurs something, steps back, looks at him, then turns and leaves. JACK watches her.

SCENE 4

St Pancras International Station, London. Arrivals. Following morning. Voiceover announcement: "This is St. Pancras International Station, London, etc." MAY'S daughter JESSICA waiting. MAY comes through customs. JESSICA waves.

MAY. Darling! How kind of you to meet me.

They embrace.

JESSICA. Are you all right, Mummy?

MAY. I feel a bit strange. Half of me is still over there in Paris.

JESSICA. Did something happen?

MAY. I met someone there.

JESSICA. A man?

MAY. Yes. A very nice man. An artist.

JESSICA. That's wonderful!

MAY. Yes, but there are complications.

JESSICA. He's married?

MAY. No, nothing like that. It's very odd. You see, he's convinced we'd met before. Years ago. And what's more he said we'd had an affair!

JESSICA. Really?

MAY. Yes. He keeps bringing it up. I didn't know what he was talking about. So, you see, I could never really trust him. He obviously had some kind of weird agenda. God knows what. So, I ... *(Her voice breaks with the emotion.)* I came back!

JESSICA. Déjà vu.

MAY. How do you mean?

JESSICA. Don't you remember? When I was a young girl - a couple of years after you and Dad broke up - you told me about a relationship you'd had earlier that summer. With an artist. In Paris.

MAY. *Did I?*

JESSICA. You were obviously in love. And you said the same thing then: you couldn't trust him.

MAY. I told you that?

JESSICA. Oh, yes. But are you sure it's him you can't trust?

MAY. What do you mean?

JESSICA. Maybe you can't trust yourself? And all those feelings that have come flooding back.

MAY. I left him in the lurch. Waiting for me. I fled. I always do that.

JESSICA. There's a Eurostar leaving for Paris in 45 minutes. Platform 3. Boarding is still open. The booking office is just over there. If you hurry ...

MAY. Thank you, darling!

She hugs JESSICA, grabs her case and hurries away towards the booking office.

JESSICA. Good luck!

MAY *(off)* Thank you!

Music over "Orange Blossom Special" harmonica J. J. Milteau

SCENE 5

Same day early afternoon. JACK'S flat. He is working at his easel. Breakfast things set out on table. Doorbell rings. JACK looks up, goes to door, opens it: MAY standing on doorstep with case.

MAY. Jack!

She falls into his arms.

JACK. May! Come in, come in.

He takes her case. She enters.

Going somewhere?

MAY. Actually I've just come back. From London.

JACK. *What!*

MAY. I did a lot of thinking in the train. And I've decided to turn over a new leaf. It's not too late, is it?

JACK. It's never too late. I'll put the kettle on.

Exit JACK to kitchen.

MAY. I was wondering, is your offer still open? About putting me up. And putting up with me.

JACK. I think we may be able to fit you in.

MAY sees portrait on wall.

MAY. You've done another portrait.

JACK. I did that one a long time ago.

MAY. Who is it? If I may ask? A girlfriend of yours?

JACK. As a matter of fact she is.

MAY *(Secretly crestfallen)* She's so beautiful!

JACK. You don't recognise her?

MAY. Should I? ... *It's not!* Is it?

He removes painting from wall, hands it to MAY.

MAY *(Reading inscription.)* "May. Paris. September 2,008." Oh!

JACK. I was sorting through some old stuff of mine last night. And I came across it. You left it behind. Sixteen years ago. So, I hung it on the wall. But then after a while seeing it every day began to upset me. So in the end I took it down and put it away.

MAY. But now I'm back.

JACK. Yes.

JACK takes her hand. They tango.

© Nick Calderbank, 2025
Édition : BoD · Books on Demand,
31 avenue Saint-Rémy, 57600 Forbach, bod@bod.fr
Impression : Libri Plureos GmbH, Friedensallee 273,
22763 Hamburg (Allemagne)
ISBN : 978-2-3225-5796-7
Dépôt légal : Janvier 2025